NURSERY
SONGS & RHYMES

Illustrated by Eric Kincaid

The Five Mile Press

The Five Mile Press Pty Ltd
950 Stud Road, Rowville
Victoria 3178, Australia
Email: publishing@fivemile.com.au
Website: www.fivemile.com.au

First published by Brimax Books Ltd, 1996
This format first published 2005

Illustrations © Eric Kincaid
This format © The Five Mile Press Pty Ltd
CD produced by Spoken Word Productions

Designed by Julie Thompson

National Library of Australia Cataloguing-in-Publication data
Nursery songs and rhymes.
For children.
ISBN 1 74124 670 9.
l. Nursery rhymes. 2. Children's songs. I. Kincaid, Eric.
398.8

CONTENTS

INTRODUCTION

Such popular nursery rhymes as 'Baa, Baa Black Sheep', 'Twinkle, Twinkle, Little Star', 'Pussy Cat, Pussy Cat', and 'Humpty Dumpty' have delighted small children for centuries. All these classic verses – and many more – can be found in this delightful collection.

Some other enchanting nursery rhymes, in danger of being forgotten by today's children, have also been included as well as a sprinkling of verses by writers such as Robert Louis Stevenson, Edward Lear and Emily Brontë.

Well-known children's book illustrator Eric Kincaid has brought these rhymes to life, conjuring up beautiful old villages, rustic scenes and a wealth of characters – both human and animal – that feature in these rhymes.

Join Little Miss Muffet, The Queen of Hearts, Simple Simon and dozens of other bewitching characters on a spellbinding journey into the magical world of rhyme and verse.

This is a book for children to treasure all their lives.

Six Little Mice

Six little mice sat down to spin;
Pussy passed by and she peeped in.
What are you doing, my little men?
Weaving coats for gentlemen.
Shall I come in and cut off your threads?
No, no, Mistress Pussy, you'd bite off our heads.
Oh no, I'll not; I'll help you to spin.
That may be so, but you don't come in.

SING A SONG OF SIXPENCE

Sing a song of sixpence,
A pocket full of rye;
Four and twenty blackbirds
Baked in a pie.

When the pie was opened,
The birds began to sing;
Wasn't that a dainty dish
To set before the king?

The king was in his counting house,
Counting out his money;
The queen was in the parlour,
Eating bread and honey.

The maid was in the garden,
Hanging out the clothes,
There came a little blackbird,
And snapped off her nose.

A CAT CAME FIDDLING

A cat came fiddling out of a barn,
With a pair of bagpipes under her arm;
She could sing nothing but fiddle-cum-fee,
The mouse has married the bumblebee.
Pipe, cat; dance, mouse;
We'll have a wedding at our good house.

LITTLE MISS MUFFET

Little Miss Muffet
Sat on a tuffet,
Eating her curds and whey;
There came a big spider,
Who sat down beside her
And frightened Miss Muffet away.

$\mathscr{I}$ SAW THREE SHIPS

I saw three ships come sailing by,
Come sailing by, come sailing by,
I saw three ships come sailing by,
On New Year's Day in the morning.

And what do you think was in them then,
Was in them then, was in them then?
And what do you think was in them then,
On New Year's Day in the morning?

Three pretty girls were in them then,
Were in them then, were in them then,
Three pretty girls were in them then,
On New Year's Day in the morning.

One could whistle, and one could sing,
And one could play on the violin;
Such joy there was at my wedding,
On New Year's Day in the morning.

RIDE A COCK-HORSE TO BANBURY CROSS

Ride a cock-horse to Banbury Cross,
To see a fine lady upon a white horse;
Rings on her fingers and bells on her toes,
And she shall have music wherever she goes.

IF ALL THE WORLD WERE PAPER

If all the world were paper,
And all the sea were ink,
If all the trees were bread and cheese,
What should we have to drink?

THERE WAS AN OLD WOMAN

There was an old woman who lived in a shoe,
She had so many children she didn't know what to do;
She gave them some broth without any bread;
She whipped them all soundly and put them to bed.

$\mathcal{I}$ SEE THE MOON

I see the moon,
And the moon sees me;
God bless the moon,
And God bless me.

THE QUEEN OF HEARTS

The Queen of Hearts
She made some tarts,
All on a summer's day;
The Knave of Hearts
He stole the tarts,
And took them clean away.

The King of Hearts
Called for the tarts,
And beat the Knave full sore;
The Knave of Hearts
Brought back the tarts,
And vowed he'd steal no more.

ROCK-A-BYE, BABY

Rock-a-bye, baby, on the tree-top,
When the wind blows the cradle will rock;
When the bough breaks the cradle will fall,
Down will come baby, cradle, and all.

THERE WAS AN OLD WOMAN

There was an old woman tossed up in a basket,
Seventeen times as high as the moon;
Where she was going I couldn't but ask it,
For in her hand she carried a broom.
Old woman, old woman, old woman, quoth I,
Where are you going to up so high?
To brush the cobwebs off the sky!
May I go with you?
Aye, by-and-by.

JACK SPRAT

Jack Sprat could eat no fat,
His wife could eat no lean,
And so between them both, you see,
They licked the platter clean.

POLLY PUT THE KETTLE ON

Polly put the kettle on,
Polly put the kettle on,
Polly put the kettle on,
We'll all have tea.

Sukey take if off again,
Sukey take it off again,
Sukey take it off again,
They've all gone away.

HUMPTY DUMPTY

Humpty dumpty sat on a wall,
Humpty dumpty had a great fall.
All the king's horses and all the king's men,
Couldn't put Humpty together again.

PETER, PETER, PUMPKIN EATER

Peter, Peter, pumpkin eater,
Had a wife and couldn't keep her;
He put her in a pumpkin shell
And there he kept her very well.

BAA, BAA, BLACK SHEEP

Baa, baa, black sheep,
Have you any wool?
Yes, sir, yes, sir,
Three bags full;
One for the master,
And one for the dame,
And one for the little boy
Who lives down the lane.

GOOSEY, GOOSEY, GANDER

Goosey, goosey gander,
Whither shall I wander?
Upstairs and downstairs
And in my lady's chamber.
There I met an old man
Who would not say his prayers.
I took him by the left leg
And threw him down the stairs.

THERE WAS A LITTLE BOY

There was a little boy went into a barn,
And lay down on some hay;
An owl came out and flew about,
And the little boy ran away.

ONE, TWO, THREE, FOUR, FIVE

One, two, three, four, five,
Once I caught a fish alive,
Six, seven, eight, nine, ten,
Then I let it go again.

Why did you let it go?
Because it bit my finger so.
Which finger did it bite?
This little finger on the right.

SIMPLE SIMON MET A PIEMAN

Simple Simon met a pieman,
Going to the fair;
Says Simple Simon to the pieman,
'Let me taste your ware.'

Says the pieman to Simple Simon,
'Show me first your penny.'
Says Simple Simon to the pieman,
'Indeed I have not any.'

Simple Simon went a-fishing,
For to catch a whale;
All the water he had got
Was in his mother's pail.

Simple Simon went to look
If plums grew on a thistle;
He pricked his fingers very much,
Which made poor Simon whistle.

He went for water in a sieve
But soon it all fell through;
And now poor Simple Simon
Bids you all adieu.

JACK AND JILL

Jack and Jill went up the hill
To fetch a pail of water;
Jack fell down and broke his crown,
And Jill came tumbling after.

Up Jack got, and home did trot,
As fast as he could caper,
To old Dame Dob, who patched his nob
With vinegar and brown paper.

$\mathcal{T}$HY CRADLE IS GREEN

Hush-a-bye baby,
Thy cradle is green,
Father's a nobleman,
Mother's a queen;
And Betty's a lady,
And wears a gold ring;
And Johnny's a drummer,
And drums for the king.

HEY DIDDLE DIDDLE

Hey diddle diddle,
The cat and the fiddle,
The cow jumped over the moon;
The little dog laughed to see such sport,
And the dish ran away with the spoon.

THIS LITTLE PIG WENT TO MARKET

This little pig went to market,
This little pig stayed home,
This little pig had roast beef,
This little pig had none,
And this little pig cried,
Wee-wee-wee-wee!
All the way home.

RIDE A COCK-HORSE

Ride a cock-horse
To Banbury Cross,
To see what Tommy can buy;
A penny white loaf,
A penny white cake,
And a two-penny apple-pie.

TWINKLE, TWINKLE, LITTLE STAR

Twinkle, twinkle, little star,
How I wonder what you are!
Up above the world so high,
Like a diamond in the sky.
Twinkle, twinkle, little star,
How I wonder what you *are*!

PAST, PRESENT AND FUTURE

Tell me, tell me, smiling child,
What the past is like to thee?
'An autumn evening soft and mild
With a wind that sighs mournfully.'

Tell me, what is the present hour?
'A green and flowery spray
Where a young bird sits gathering its power
To mount and fly away.'

And what is the future, happy one?
'A sea beneath a cloudless sun;
A mighty, glorious, dazzling sea
Stretching to infinity.'

Emily Brontë

OH WHERE, OH WHERE HAS MY LITTLE DOG GONE?

Oh where, oh where has my little dog gone?
Oh where, oh where can he be?
With his ears cut short and his tail cut long,
Oh where, oh where is he?

PUSSY CAT MOLE

Pussy Cat Mole jumped over a coal
And in her best petticoat burnt a great hole.
Poor pussy's weeping, she'll have no more milk
Until her best petticoat's mended with silk.

SEE-SAW, MARGERY DAW

See-saw, Margery Daw,
Jacky shall have a new master;
Jacky shall have but a penny a day,
Because he can't work any faster.

LITTLE POLLY FLINDERS

Little Polly Flinders
Sat among the cinders,
Warming her pretty little toes;
Her mother came and caught her,
And whipped her little daughter
For spoiling her nice new clothes.

THIS IS THE HOUSE THAT JACK BUILT

This is the house that Jack built.

This is the malt
That lay in the house that Jack built.

This is the rat,
That ate the malt
That lay in the house that Jack built.

This is the cat,
That killed the rat,
That ate the malt
That lay in the house that Jack built.

This is the dog,
That worried the cat,
That killed the rat,
That ate the malt
That lay in the house that Jack built.

This is the cow with the crumpled horn,
That tossed the dog,
That worried the cat,
That killed the rat,
That ate the malt
That lay in the house that Jack built.

This is the maiden all forlorn,
That milked the cow with the
   crumpled horn,
That tossed the dog,
That worried the cat,
That killed the rat,
That ate the malt,
That lay in the house that Jack built.

This is the man all tattered and torn,
That kissed the maiden all forlorn,
That milked the cow with the
    crumpled horn,
That tossed the dog,
That worried the cat,
That killed the rat,
That ate the malt,
That lay in the house that Jack built.

This is the priest all shaven and shorn,
That married the man all tattered and torn,
That kissed the maiden all forlorn,
That milked the cow with the crumpled horn,
That tossed the dog,
That worried the cat,
That killed the rat,
That ate the malt,
That lay in the house that Jack built.

This is the cock that crowed in the morn,
That waked the priest all shaven and shorn,
That married the man all tattered and torn,
That kissed the maiden all forlorn,
That milked the cow with the crumpled horn,
That tossed the dog,
That worried the cat,
That killed the rat,
That ate the malt,
That lay in the house that Jack built.

This is the farmer sowing his corn,
That kept the cock that crowed in the morn,
That waked the priest all shaven and shorn,
That married the man all tattered and torn,
That kissed the maiden all forlorn,
That milked the cow with the crumpled horn,
That tossed the dog,
That worried the cat,
That killed the rat,
That ate the malt,
That lay in the house that Jack built.

LITTLE BO-PEEP

Little Bo-Peep has lost her sheep,
And can't tell where to find them;
Leave them alone, and they'll come home,
And bring their tails behind them.

Little Bo-Peep fell fast asleep,
And dreamt she heard them bleating;
And when she awoke, she found it a joke,
For they were still all fleeting.

Then up she took her little crook,
Determined for to find them;
She found them indeed, but it made her heart bleed,
For they'd left their tails behind them.

It happened one day, as Bo-Peep did stray
Into a meadow hard by,
There she espied their tails side by side,
All hung on a tree to dry.

She heaved a sigh, and wiped her eye,
Then went o'er hill and dale,
And tried what she could, as a shepherdess should,
To tack to each sheep its tail.

HOW MANY MILES TO BABYLON?

How many miles to Babylon?
Three score miles and ten.
Can I get there by candlelight?
Yes, and back again.
If your heels are nimble and light,
You may get there by candlelight.

HOT CROSS BUNS!

Hot cross buns!
Hot cross buns!
One a penny, two a penny,
Hot cross buns!
If your daughters do not like them
Give them to your sons;
But if you haven't any of these pretty little elves
You cannot do better than eat them all yourselves.

TWO LITTLE DICKY BIRDS

Two little dicky birds
Sitting on a wall;
One named Peter,
The other named Paul.

Fly away, Peter!
Fly away, Paul!

Come back, Peter!
Come back, Paul!

Pussy cat, pussy cat

Pussy cat, pussy cat, where have you been?
I've been to London to look at the Queen.
Pussy cat, pussy cat, what did you there?
I frightened a little mouse under her chair.

THERE WAS AN OLD WOMAN

There was an old woman
Lived under a hill,
And if she's not gone
She lives there still.

LITTLE BOY BLUE

Little Boy Blue
Come blow your horn,
The sheep's in the meadow,
The cow's in the corn.
But where is the boy
Who looks after the sheep?
He's under a haystack,
Fast asleep.
Will you wake him?
No, not I,
For if I do,
He's sure to cry.

MARY, MARY, QUITE CONTRARY

Mary, Mary, quite contrary,
How does your garden grow?
With silver bells and cockleshells,
And pretty maids all in a row.

RING-A-RING O'ROSES

Ring-a-ring o'roses,
A pocket full of posies,
A-tishoo! A-tishoo!
We all fall down.

THREE LITTLE KITTENS

Three little kittens they lost their mittens,
And they began to cry,
Oh, mother dear, we sadly fear
That we have lost our mittens.
What! Lost your mittens, you naughty kittens!
Then you shall have no pie.
Meow, meow, meow.
No, you shall have no pie.

The three little kittens they found
  their mittens,
And they began to cry,
Oh, mother dear, see here, see here,
For we have found our mittens.
Put on your mittens, you silly kittens,
And you shall have some pie.
Purr-r, purr-r, purr-r.
Oh, let us have some pie.

The three little kittens put on their mittens,
And soon ate up the pie;
Oh, mother dear, we greatly fear
That we have soiled our mittens.
What! Soiled your mittens, you naughty kittens!
Then they began to sigh,
Meow, meow, meow.
Then they began to sigh.

The three little kittens they washed their mittens,
And hung them out to dry;
Oh! mother dear, do you not hear
That we have washed our mittens?
What! Washed your mittens, then you're good kittens,
But I smell a rat close by.
Meow, meow, meow.
We smell a rat close by.

THERE WAS A CROOKED MAN

There was a crooked man, and he walked a crooked mile,
He found a crooked sixpence against a crooked stile;
He bought a crooked cat, which caught a crooked mouse,
And they all lived together in a little crooked house.

WEE WILLIE WINKIE

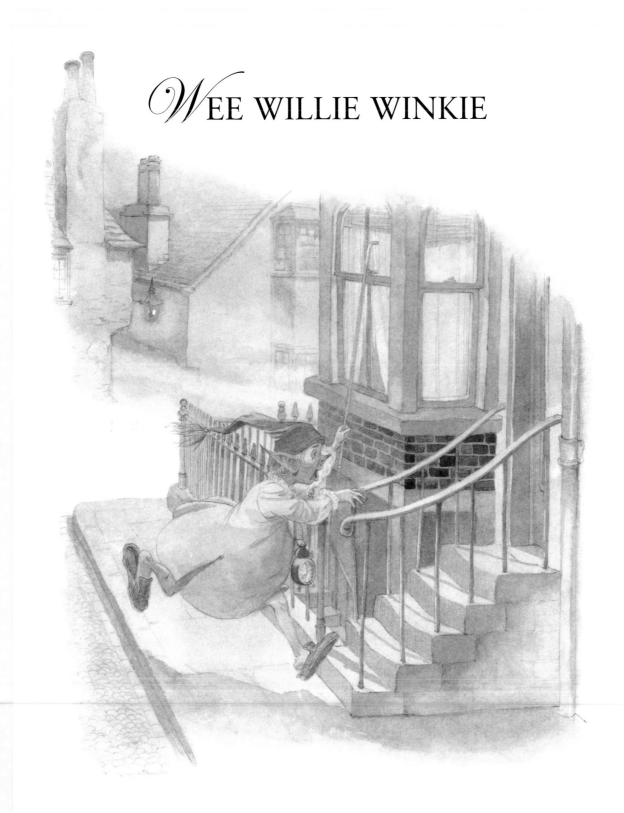

Wee Willie Winkie runs through the town,
Upstairs and downstairs in his nightgown.
Rapping at the window, crying through the lock,
Are the children all in bed, for now it's eight o'clock.

THE TABLE AND THE CHAIR

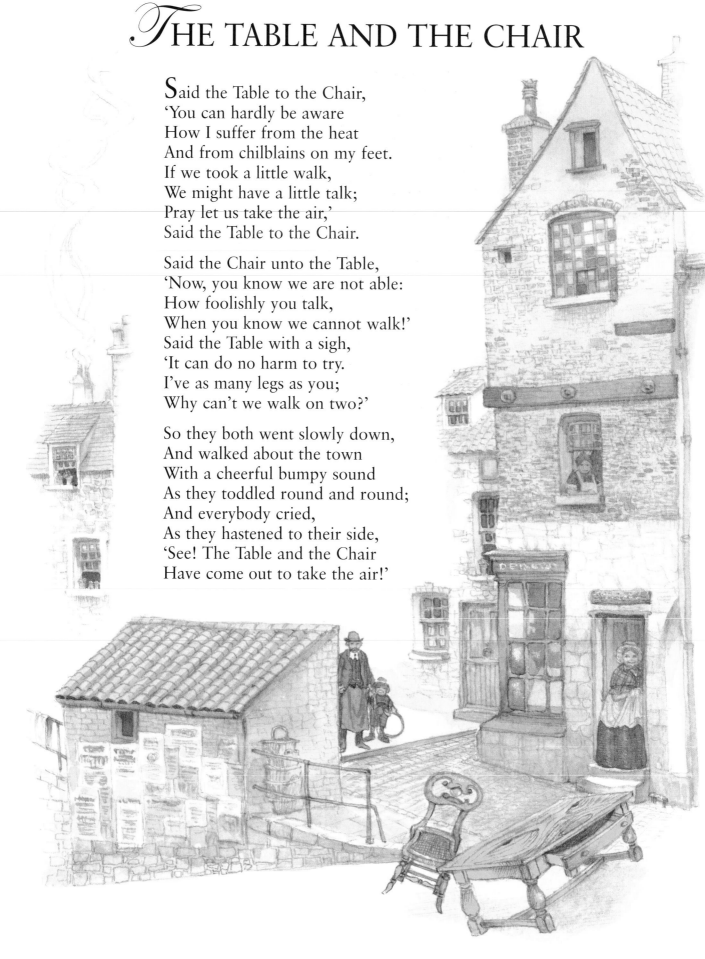

Said the Table to the Chair,
'You can hardly be aware
How I suffer from the heat
And from chilblains on my feet.
If we took a little walk,
We might have a little talk;
Pray let us take the air,'
Said the Table to the Chair.

Said the Chair unto the Table,
'Now, you know we are not able:
How foolishly you talk,
When you know we cannot walk!'
Said the Table with a sigh,
'It can do no harm to try.
I've as many legs as you;
Why can't we walk on two?'

So they both went slowly down,
And walked about the town
With a cheerful bumpy sound
As they toddled round and round;
And everybody cried,
As they hastened to their side,
'See! The Table and the Chair
Have come out to take the air!'

But in going down an alley
To a castle in a valley,
They completely lost their way,
And they wandered all the day;
Till, to see them safely back,
They paid a Ducky-quack,
And a Beetle and a Mouse,
Who took them to their house.

Then they whispered to each other,
'O delightful little brother,
What a lovely walk we've taken!
Let us dine on beans and bacon.'
So the Ducky and the leetle
Browny-Mousy and the Beetle
Dined and danced upon their heads
Till they toddled to their beds.

Edward Lear

THE MOON

The moon has a face like the clock in the hall;
She shines on thieves and on the garden wall,
On streets and fields and harbour quays,
And birdies asleep in the forks of the trees.

The squalling cat and the squeaking mouse,
The howling dog by the door of the house,
That bat that lies in bed at noon,
All love to be out by the light of the moon.

But all of the things that belong to the day
Cuddle to sleep to be out of her way;
And flowers and children close their eyes
Till up in the morning the sun shall rise.

Robert Louis Stevenson

THE WIND

I saw you toss the kites on high
And blow the birds about the sky;
And all around I heard you pass,
Like ladies' skirts across the grass –
    O wind, a-blowing all day long,
    O wind, that sings so loud a song!

I saw the different things you did,
But always you yourself you hid.
I felt you push, I heard you call,
I could not see yourself at all –
    O wind, a-blowing all day long,
    O wind, that sings so loud a song.

O you that are so strong and cold,
O blower, are you young or old?
Are you a beast of field and tree,
Or just a stronger child than me?
    O wind, a blowing all day long,
    O wind, that sings so loud a song!

Robert Louis Stevenson